MERCER MAYER'S
LC + THE CRITTER KIDS®

P9-CEF-523

# LITTLE SHOP OF MAGIC

Written by Erica Farber / J. R. Sansevere

**A Golden Book • New York**

Western Publishing Company, Inc., Racine, Wisconsin 53404

A Mercer Mayer Ltd./J. R. Sansevere Book

LC

VELVET

LITTLE SISTER

TIGER

KOOL BEAR

SLICK RICK

SU SU     GABBY     TIMOTHY

GATOR     FLEX     HENRIETTA

# CHAPTER 1

# THE HUNT

The sun was setting. It looked like a red ball, sinking slowly behind the trees. The sky was turning the deep violet-blue of twilight as the last rays of sunlight streaked the field where the Critter Kids were playing baseball.

Actually, the field wasn't a field. It was a vacant lot, bordered by woods, at the end of Green Frog Lane.

LC was at bat. His dog, Yo Yo, was lying near home

◀ 1 ▶

plate, scratching his ear. Tiger was pitching. Henrietta was catching. Velvet was on first base. Su Su was on second. Gator was on third. And Gabby and Timothy were in the outfield.

Tiger stepped up to the pitcher's mound as the first stars began to twinkle in the sky.

"Last pitch!" called Gabby. "It's almost time to go home!"

"Get ready!" LC called back. "This one's gonna be a home run!"

Yo Yo stood up and barked in agreement.

"Right," said Su Su to Velvet. "LC's been saying that all afternoon."

LC got into his batting stance. Tiger went into his windup and threw a fastball right up the middle. Whack! LC connected with the ball and it went flying up in the air. It soared right over Gabby's and Timothy's heads before disappearing into the woods.

"Yes!" exclaimed LC, jumping up and down.

"Okay, the game's over," said Su Su, throwing down her mitt. "I'm going home to manicure my nails. All the polish chipped off because of this stupid mitt."

"I've got to go, too," said Gator.

"Me, too," said Tiger, Timothy, and Velvet.

"It's time for my bedtime snack," said Henrietta. "Chocolate chip cookies and a banana shake. Yum-yum!"

"How can you eat all that before you go to sleep?" asked Velvet. "Chocolate always gives me nightmares."

"Doesn't bother me," said Henrietta, taking off across the field. "See you guys tomorrow."

"Hey, what about my ball?" asked Gabby. "I've got to get it."

"I'll come with you," said LC. "After all, I am the slugger who hit it right out of the park."

"We better hurry," said Gabby. "It's getting dark."

LC and Gabby headed into the woods. The trees cast weird shadows in the dim light. And Gabby and LC had to move very slowly so they wouldn't trip over the vines and brambles that grew wild there.

Yo Yo ran ahead of them, leading the way. Suddenly he began to growl.

"That's strange," said LC. "Yo Yo never growls."

"He probably just saw a rabbit or something," said Gabby matter-of-factly. "You know how dumb dogs are."

"Yo Yo's not dumb," said LC. "And I'm telling you, he never growls at anything. Why, he's probably the nicest dog in all of Critterville." LC cupped his hands around his mouth. "Yo Yo!" he called. "Where are you, boy?"

Just then they came to a clearing. A big yellow moon was beginning to rise behind the trees. And there was Yo Yo standing in the center of the clearing, his tail down, and his body coiled as if ready to spring at something.

"Grrr!" growled Yo Yo.

All of a sudden LC and Gabby heard the leaves rustling around them.

LC felt his scalp prickle.

"Do you feel like somebody is watching us?" whispered Gabby.

LC gulped and nodded as strange panting and snorting noises filled the air. He and Gabby looked at each other, their eyes wide.

"What's that?" whispered LC.

Gabby didn't answer. She just pointed. All around them, glowing in the darkness, were red and yellow eyes. Gabby and LC strained to make out the silhouettes of some very unusual-looking creatures.

"They've got us surrounded," whispered LC. "Don't move."

"What are they?" Gabby whispered back.

"I can't tell," said LC. "It's too dark. Maybe wild pigs."

"Wild pigs in Critterville?" said Gabby. "I don't think so."

Just then they heard the sound of a horse whinnying behind them. LC and Gabby jumped. There in the moonlight was a huge gray and white stallion, rearing its front legs high in the air.

"Whoa, Equus!" yelled the rider. He was dressed in a red riding outfit, long black boots, and a black hat.

The horse quieted instantly.

"*Backus omnus canus nichtus!*" the man shouted.

Suddenly all the eyes disappeared as the creatures, whatever they were, quickly vanished back into the woods.

"Phew!" sighed LC in relief.

"Sorry about that," said the man. "My, er, dogs get a bit wild when they're on the hunt."

"Hunt?" said Gabby, staring at the man, who was holding a riding crop with a tiny skull on the end of it.

"Yes," he answered with a strange smile. "I always hunt at night. It's the best time to catch things unawares, don't you think?"

"Uh . . . I guess so," said LC, shifting uncomfortably. "Well, we've gotta go."

"I believe I have something that belongs to you, mademoiselle," continued the man, holding out Gabby's baseball.

"Gee, thanks," said Gabby. She quickly grabbed her ball from the man's hand.

"Well, I must be off," said the man, hitting Equus with his crop. "The night waits for no man." He laughed loudly as he galloped away.

"I have just one question," said Gabby. "How did he know that the ball was mine?"

"Beats me," said LC. "Let's go!"

And without another word, Gabby and LC took off through the woods with Yo Yo at their heels. LC didn't stop running until he was all the way home, and his heart didn't stop pounding until he was safely in his bed under the covers.

# CHAPTER 2

# IT'S MAGIC!

The next day was Saturday. LC and the Critter Kids were sitting in the food court at the Critter Mall. There was a large cheese pizza on their table.

"*Mmm!*" said LC, licking his lips. "Pizza is the perfect food!"

"Yeah," agreed Tiger as he, LC, and Gator each grabbed a slice from the sizzling pie and began to stuff it into their mouths. Trickles of tomato sauce dribbled down their chins.

"Hot!" they all tried to yell.

"Why don't you guys just wait till it cools off?" said Gabby. "You look disgusting."

LC, Tiger, and Gator just looked at her and kept on wolfing down their slices.

"They always do that," said Su Su, shaking her head. "It's a guy thing."

"No, it's not," said Henrietta, picking up another one of the sizzling slices and shoving it into her mouth. "It's a food thing. If you're a gourmet like myself, you know pizza is best when it's so hot it burns the roof of your mouth."

"So, what are we going to do?" asked Velvet, changing the subject. "We don't have to meet my mom for another hour."

"Let's go to the arcade," said Tiger. "I've got a whole bunch of quarters."

"What about the baseball card store?" suggested Gator. "I wanna trade some old cards for some new rookie cards."

"Oh, no," said Su Su. "We've got to go to Blueberries. They're having a big sale on earrings."

"We always do the same stuff every weekend," said LC. "Why can't we do something different? Something *exciting*."

Since no one could decide what to do, the Critter Kids finally figured they would start at the top level of the mall and work their way down, looking for something interesting. When they were finished with their pizza and had thrown away the garbage, LC led the way through the crowds of Saturday afternoon shoppers toward the escalator. Just as he was about to get on the steps, he spotted a store he had never seen before. His eyes lit up and a smile spread across his face.

"You guys!" he called, turning around. "Look over there!" He pointed to the left.

"Hey, kid, move it!" someone yelled from the long line of critters behind him. "We don't have all day."

LC walked toward the store. The Critter Kids all shrugged and followed.

"Little Shop of Magic," said Tiger, reading the unusual and old-fashioned sign hanging above the store.

"I've never seen this store before," said Gabby.

"It must be new," said Velvet.

"It sure doesn't look new to me," said Su Su, peering through the window into the dim, dusty interior of the store.

"And it sure doesn't look open," said Gator.

"Look at all this cool stuff," said LC, staring at the merchandise in the window. He read the label on a large red cone: "Amaze your friends with this disappearing cone. Whatever you put under the cone will vanish without a trace."

"And look at that weird glass," Gabby said. She pointed to a crystal goblet and read the label: "For nonbelievers who don't think that ghosts exist, conjure up a specter with just one shake of the glass."

"Wow! We've got to go into this store," said LC.

Tiger tried to open the door. "It's locked," he said. "Guess it's closed."

"It can't be closed," said LC.

"It *is* closed," Gabby said, rattling the doorknob.

"Let's go," said Su Su. "We've only got forty-five minutes left and there's so much to buy."

Su Su and Gabby and the rest of the Critter Kids turned around and started walking back toward the escalator. LC decided to try the door one more time. But no sooner had he reached for the brass door handle than the door suddenly swung open—all by itself!

LC jumped. His eyes opened wide as he gazed into the murky depths of the store. He noticed a statue of a lion that bobbed its head up and down, almost as if it were alive. He also saw a shield of shiny silver that claimed to protect its wearer from any harm.

And so many more great things LC wished that he could have . . . just *had* to have. . . .

Without another thought, LC disappeared inside the Little Shop of Magic. And the door slammed shut behind him.

# CHAPTER 3

# ABRACADABRA!

LC's eyes opened wider and wider as he looked around at all the incredible things that filled the Little Shop of Magic. There was a bloody finger in a jar and crystal balls in a bowl and glasses that claimed to give their wearer X-ray vision. And one mirror that made LC's body look tall and thin, and another that made him look short and fat.

*"Hel-lo-o!"* LC called out.

There was no answer.

He walked over to the counter. "Hello!"

he called again, this time a bit more loudly.

But there was only dead silence. It didn't seem as if anybody was in the store at all. LC knew he should leave, but the urge to stay was overpowering.

He spotted a ceramic statue of a monkey that held out cards in its hands. He picked up a card. "L. B. Strangely, Proprietor, Little Shop of Magic . . . Genuine magic guaranteed," he read aloud.

"May I help you?" said a strange voice that seemed to come out of nowhere.

LC turned around. He couldn't see anybody. His heart was pounding as he backed up toward the door.

Just then there was a loud rapping sound right behind him. "Aaahhh!" LC screamed.

He turned around. And there were the rest of the Critter Kids clustered around the window, peering into the shop.

"Your friends, I presume," the strange voice said.

Just as LC was about to run out of the shop, the door swung open by itself again and the Critter Kids walked in.

"Hey, you're the guy we saw last night!" exclaimed Gabby, staring at someone behind LC.

LC turned around. And where there hadn't been a single soul before was the same man he and Gabby had seen on the gray and white horse with the dogs.

Now that LC could get a closer look at him, he noticed that the man's skin was very pale, almost bloodless, and that his eyes were a strange shade of green flecked with yellow—almost like a cat's eyes.

"My name is L. B. Strangely," said the man. "Welcome to the Little Shop of Magic. I believe your friend here," he said, pointing to LC, "is quite ready for some magic. Are you not?"

LC didn't say anything. He just stared at L. B. Strangely. His mouth opened and closed, but no words came out.

"Cat got your tongue?" continued L. B. Strangely, sauntering over to LC with a strange half-smile on his face. "Or should I say, rabbit?" And with one quick sweep of his long arm, L. B. Strangely pulled a rabbit out from under LC's baseball cap.

"Wow!" breathed Tiger. "That was awesome."

"How did you do that?" asked Henrietta.

"Magic," said L. B. Strangely, dropping the rabbit onto the floor. The rabbit hopped away behind the counter.

"There's no such thing as magic," said Gabby.

"Then how do you explain this?" asked L. B. Strangely. He stretched out his long fingers, and suddenly the most beautiful fireworks exploded off his fingertips.

The Critter Kids stared at the lights. They were mesmerizing.

"Incredible!" gasped Velvet.

"Unbelievable!" exclaimed Gator.

"It's just an optical illusion that fools the naked eye," said Timothy. "There's a scientific explanation for all of this."

"Really?" said L. B. Strangely, moving over to Timothy. "I believe you will find an egg in your pocket. Could you hand it to me, please?"

Timothy reached into his pocket. His eyes opened wide as he pulled out a large, odd-looking egg. He handed it to L. B. Strangely without a word.

"How did that get there?" asked Su Su.

For once Timothy had nothing to say.

Then with another sweeping motion, L. B. Strangely produced a wand. "This is a magic wand," he explained. "Watch this." He tapped the egg with the wand. "Now the egg will break open."

The Critter Kids stared at the egg as it

cracked open.

"A creature long believed to be extinct will come out," continued L. B. Strangely.

A pointy green snout suddenly broke through the shell.

The Critter Kids gulped as a scaly creature emerged.

"What is it?" whispered Velvet.

"A velociraptor, of course," answered L. B. Strangely. "One of the most fearsome dinosaurs of the Jurassic period, I believe."

"What?!" said Gabby. "A dinosaur! It can't be real."

"It's magic, remember?" said L. B. Strangely. "Now watch this. With a few more taps of my wand, this baby will grow into a full-size adult raptor."

"That's impossible!" shouted Timothy, pushing his glasses higher up on his nose.

L. B. Strangely didn't respond. Instead he simply tapped the baby dinosaur with his

wand, and right before everyone's eyes it grew bigger and bigger until it was almost as tall as L. B. Strangely himself. The dinosaur took one look at the Critter Kids and began to roar so loudly that everything in the shop rattled.

"Thank you very much, raptor," said L. B. Strangely to the dinosaur. "Now I think it's time for you to return to your egg."

The Critter Kids watched in amazement as L. B. Strangely tapped the big dinosaur a few more times with his wand. The creature returned to its baby size and then disappeared back inside the egg.

"Enough magic for one day," L. B. Strangely told the Critter Kids, whose mouths were all open wide in disbelief. "The shop is closed."

Before they knew it, the Critter Kids found themselves back outside the store, with no memory at all of how they got there.

# CHAPTER 4

# GARGOYLE OF GREED

Later that afternoon LC and the Critter Kids were in their clubhouse. It was actually a barn that had once been the Critters' garage, but LC and his friends had turned it into their clubhouse. They always went there to discuss anything important— and their experience with L. B. Strangely had left them with quite a bit to talk about.

"I'm telling you, there's only one word for guys like that," said Su Su, trying on one of the new pairs of earrings she had bought. "And that's *w-a-c-k-o*—wacko."

"Maybe," agreed Henrietta, popping a chocolate-covered cherry into her mouth, "but you gotta admit those tricks he did were pretty cool."

"Yeah," agreed Gator. "They were the best magic tricks I've ever seen, especially that dinosaur one."

"I think so, too," said Tiger.

"Me, too," said Velvet.

"I just don't understand how he did all those tricks," said Gabby, pacing back and forth. "It was creepy."

"Simple," said LC. "Magic."

"But there's no such thing as magic," Timothy pointed out. "There's a scientific explanation for everything he did."

"Like what?" asked LC, putting both of his feet up on the table and opening the new *Spider Critter* comic he had bought at the mall.

"I don't know," said Timothy, flipping a page in one of the big science textbooks he always carried in his briefcase, "but I'm going to figure it out."

"Hey!" said Gabby. "What's that on the bottom of your shoe?" She pointed to one of LC's sneakers.

There was a small rectangular card, about the size of a playing card, stuck to a wad of purple bubble gum on the bottom of his sneaker. Everybody watched as LC pulled off the card.

On the front of the card was a picture of a ferocious-looking winged monster. Its tongue was sticking out of its mouth, and there was an evil expression on its half-bird, half-demon face. Each corner of the card had a picture of a gemstone. One was a ruby, another was an emerald, a third was a diamond, and the fourth was a sapphire. Weird lettering was hand-printed on the back of the card: SWYN . . . GARGOYLE OF GREED.

All the Critter Kids except Timothy gathered around LC to look at the card.

"What's a gargoyle?" asked Gator.

"A grotesque human or animal form usually carved as a waterspout on a building or a fountain," explained Timothy, without looking up from his science book.

"Where did you get that card?" Tiger asked.

"It must have gotten stuck to my shoe somewhere in the mall," said LC.

"I bet it's from that Little Shop of Magic," said Gabby.

"I didn't see any cards like that when we were there," said LC.

Gabby stared at the card. "You know what this gargoyle thing reminds me of?" she asked.

"What?" said LC.

"Those weird dogs we saw last night in the woods," Gabby said.

"Give me a break," said LC, shaking his head. Gabby was always letting her imagination run away with her. "Gargoyles are stone statues. They're not alive."

"Aha!" Timothy suddenly exclaimed, looking up from his textbook. "I've got it! I think I know just how L. B. Strangely did those tricks."

"How?" asked Tiger.

"He *didn't*," Timothy said.

"Huh?" said Henrietta, popping another chocolate-covered cherry into her mouth.

"He simply hypnotized us with those colored lights, using holographic images and reflecting them off mirrors," explained Timothy. "Then he told us that a dinosaur was hatching and growing right in front of us. Because we were hypnotized, we believed him and thought we saw what he was telling us, but in actuality there was never a dinosaur or egg at all."

"Whoa, dude!" said Tiger. "That's too deep for me."

"Maybe you're right," said Gabby, slowly. "That would explain it. But there was still something very strange about that guy, if you ask me. And that card, too."

Meanwhile, on the other side of town at the Critter Mall, all the stores were closing for the night. The night watchman was walking down the aisles to make sure that no shoppers were left. His footsteps echoed down the empty corridors.

Over in the Little Shop of Magic, L. B. Strangely was in his back room. He was seated at an old-fashioned wooden table with claw legs. On top of the table was a deck of cards, some tall wax candles, and sparkling gemstones of many colors. And all around him were stone gargoyles of different shapes and sizes.

Slowly L. B. Strangely drew a card from the top of the deck and laid it faceup in the top left corner of the table. A picture of a grotesque gargoyle was on the front, with smaller pictures of different gemstones in each corner. L. B. Strangely lit a candle and murmured a strange incantation. Then he put a green stone in the corner of the card

where there was a picture of an emerald, a blue stone where there was a picture of a sapphire, a red stone where there was a picture of a ruby, and a clear stone where there was a picture of a diamond. The candles cast flickering shadows around the room, making the gargoyles look almost as if they were alive.

Suddenly the stones on the corners of the card appeared to glow brighter and brighter, as if they were on fire. Seconds later something rustled softly in the half-darkness.

L. B. Strangely smiled an evil smile and proceeded to place the remaining cards in different positions all over the table. Sometimes he placed a card facedown and sometimes he placed a card faceup. Each time he placed one faceup, he lit a candle and put different stones on top of the card until the table was covered with cards and stones—except for a small space in the center.

L. B. Strangely was about to lay out the last card when he discovered that none was left. He frowned. He looked under the table, then got up, and searched the room. His pale face flushed crimson with anger. He banged the table with his fist.

"Swyn must be returned to the pack tonight!" cried L. B. Strangely. His cold, evil voice echoed through the shadowy room filled with gargoyles. "Or else!"

Then he blew out all the candles, plunging the room into total darkness.

# CHAPTER 5

# SPECIAL REPORT

Late that night a storm blew into Critterville. Thunder crashed and lightning lit up the sky. Through the pouring rain marched a strange army of gray-skinned, demonic-looking gargoyles. The stone statues had come to life! They panted and snorted as they ran through the streets of the town, their eyes glowing red and yellow.

They moved swiftly down Main Street and then turned onto Green Frog Lane. Their pace quickened as they got closer and closer to LC's house. As soon as they reached it, one of the gargoyles threw its body against the front door.

The door swung open. Rain dashed into the house as the head gargoyle stretched out a razor-sharp claw and reached for something on the table in the hall.

Upstairs in his bedroom, LC bolted upright in bed. "Oh, no!" he said. "The gargoyles are coming!"

At the same time, Yo Yo growled. He paced back and forth in front of LC's bedroom door.

LC looked around his room. He listened to the sound of the rain pattering against his window. He rubbed his eyes. "I guess I was just dreaming," he murmured. "But, boy, it sure felt real."

Before he knew it, LC was fast asleep again.

When LC woke up the next morning, the sun was streaming through his window. He yawned and stretched and went downstairs for breakfast. No one else was up yet. He poured himself a bowl of cereal.

Just then there was a knock on the back door, and Gabby came flying into the kitchen. "Turn on the TV!" she yelled. "You're not going to believe this!"

LC yawned again. "What are you talking about?" he asked sleepily.

"I'll show you," said Gabby, pulling him out of his chair and into the living room. She flipped on the TV.

"We would like to repeat this news flash," the announcer said. "Late last night there were multiple robberies at the Critter

Mall. Thousands of dollars in gemstones, including rubies, emeralds, diamonds, and sapphires, were stolen from every jewelry store in the mall except for the Gem Connection, located in the center of the mall. These thefts follow the robbery of the jewelry store on Main Street in downtown Critterville. But unlike what happened on Main Street, this time there was an eyewitness, a night watchman, who is currently in a state of shock. He will only say that he saw a bunch of wild animals that might have been dogs racing through the mall. If you have any information that could lead to the capture of these tricky thieves, please contact the Critterville Police at once."

"Who is the one person we know who has a bunch of wild animals?" Gabby asked LC.

LC looked at her. "I don't know," he said, with a shrug.

"L. B. Strangely, that's who," said Gabby. "On top of that, there were never any jewelry store robberies until he came to town."

"That could just be a coincidence," said LC. "We don't have any proof."

"Yes, we do," said Gabby. "We have that card you found yesterday. I know that's some kind of clue. Where is it?"

"I left it on the hall table," said LC.

Gabby and LC walked into the hallway just as Mr. and Mrs. Critter and Little Sister came down the stairs. The front door was wide open, and puddles were on the floor.

"LC!" said Mrs. Critter. "Why is the front door open?"

"I don't know," said LC.

"Must have blown open in the storm, dear," said Mr. Critter.

"I guess you're right," said Mrs. Critter.

"That was a quite a nasty storm we had last night."

"Hey," said LC, looking through the stack of mail and magazines on the table. "What happened to the card I put here yesterday?"

"I don't know," said Mrs. Critter. "Now you see why I'm always telling you to put your things away."

"Did you take it?" LC asked Little Sister.

"I don't know anything about some dumb card," said Little Sister. Then she marched into the kitchen.

"I know I left it here last night," said LC to Gabby.

"Hmm," said Gabby, slowly. "Our first piece of evidence is mysteriously missing. It sounds to me like someone didn't want us to have that card—someone like L. B. Strangely."

"That's crazy," said LC. "Just about anything could have happened to that card. Like it could have been thrown away. Or Yo Yo could have chewed it up. Or—"

"Think about this for a minute," interrupted Gabby as she chewed on her fingernails. "The jewelry store on Main Street is robbed the same night we see L. B. Strangely in the woods with some weird creatures he tells us are dogs. The next night there are jewelry robberies in the mall where L. B. Strangely's store just happens to be, and someone spots weird creatures that might be dogs. You find a card with a strange creature called a gargoyle on the front that looks suspiciously like one of the creatures we saw in the woods. Your front door is mysteriously wide open the next morning and the gargoyle card is missing. Need I say more?"

Suddenly LC remembered his dream about the gargoyles coming to his house. But that was just a dream. And Gabby was just playing detective and looking for mysteries the way she always did.

"Gabby, that's not real evidence," said LC firmly. "And we're not in the middle of a mystery."

"Oh, yes, we are," said Gabby. "There's only one thing to do. We have to go down to the police station pronto. And tell Sergeant Pokey everything we know."

# CHAPTER 6

# ON THE CASE

Later that morning at the police station in downtown Critterville, all the phones were ringing. Sergeant Pokey looked at the phones and shook his head. Everyone was calling to complain about the robberies, but nobody seemed to have any evidence that could help lead to the capture of the thieves.

Sergeant Pokey walked into his office and closed the door. He sat down at his desk to have his midmorning snack. He took an anchovy-and-banana sandwich out of his lunch box. In all his years on the Critterville force, he had never experienced a crisis like this one. He sighed. For the first time in his life, he didn't even feel like having his favorite snack.

Just then his phone rang. Sergeant Pokey picked it up. "Sergeant Pokey," said the Sergeant into the receiver. "Uh-huh . . . you don't say . . . uh-huh . . . well, okay . . . send them in. Thank you, Deputy."

Sergeant Pokey hung up the phone as Gabby and LC burst into his office.

"Sergeant," began Gabby, "we have some valuable information that we're sure can help you crack all these robbery cases."

And before Sergeant Pokey could even say a word, Gabby told him about L. B. Strangely and the Little Shop of Magic and LC's gargoyle card and everything that had happened in the last two days. When she finally finished speaking, Sergeant Pokey shook his head.

"So, you're telling me," said Sergeant Pokey, scratching his chin, "that some magician and some stone gargoyle statues robbed all these jewelry stores? I must say, young lady, that is one mighty tall tale."

"See," said LC to Gabby. "I told you we didn't have any evidence."

"Listen," continued Gabby, without missing a beat, "I know what you should do. You and your men should stake out the

magic shop tonight. I'm telling you it's the only way to catch L. B. Strangely in the act. And you will. Call it my detective instinct."

Just then the phone rang again. "Sergeant Pokey," the Sergeant answered. Suddenly he sat up straighter in his chair. "Uh, yes, Chief. Yes, sir. I'm on it right now. I'm working on some very solid leads as we speak. . . . "

Sergeant Pokey held the phone away from his ear. LC and Gabby listened to the angry voice shouting orders at the other end. "So, Pokey, you've got till tomorrow morning to catch these thieves, do you hear me?" the Chief bellowed. "The whole town of Critterville is going crazy over these robberies and it's got to stop. I want those hoodlums booked and in jail by tomorrow A.M. Good-bye!"

◀ 48 ▶

Sergeant Pokey hung up the phone. He looked at Gabby and LC. "Well, kids," he said, "it looks like we'll be staking out the Little Shop of Magic tonight, after all."

"Can we come?" asked Gabby.

Sergeant Pokey frowned. Then he sighed and frowned again. "Well," he finally said, "if your parents think it's okay, I guess so. But remember, this is official police business so you'll have to stay out of the way."

LC and Gabby nodded. Then they hurried home from the police station to get ready for the big night ahead.

# CHAPTER 7

# THE STAKEOUT

At eight o'clock sharp, after the Critter Mall had closed for the night, four squad cars and three motorcycles pulled into the parking lot. LC and Gabby followed Sergeant Pokey and the other officers into the mall. LC looked around. The whole place was dark, empty, and quiet.

Sergeant Pokey motioned for everybody to stop in the mall's center court.

"How are you going to set up your men?" Gabby asked Sergeant Pokey. "Because I have a really good idea. I think they should all hide in garbage cans that have been placed strategically, of course. That way, the men can jump out and take the thieves by surprise. And we can hide behind the cans and watch the whole thing. Here, I drew a diagram to show you."

Gabby handed Sergeant Pokey a piece of paper.

"Now, see here, young lady," said Sergeant Pokey. "I'm not putting my men in the trash, and that's final."

"Pokey!" an angry voice boomed from behind them. "What's your plan? I want to see a diagram showing where all the men are going to be positioned right now!"

The Chief marched up to them and frowned at Sergeant Pokey. "Well," he boomed. "You *do* have a diagram, don't you?"

Without batting an eye, Sergeant Pokey handed Gabby's diagram to the Chief.

All eyes were on the Chief as he studied the piece of paper. He did not stop frowning once.

"Good thinking, Pokey," the Chief finally said, returning the diagram to Sergeant Pokey. "The old garbage-can trick. I just saw that in a rerun of *Critter Vice*. It works every time. Well, good luck."

With that the Chief strode away and disappeared from the mall.

A short while later, all the officers were positioned in garbage cans near the Little Shop of Magic. Gabby, LC, and Sergeant Pokey were hiding behind three of the garbage cans by the shop.

LC peered into the darkness. All was quiet in the mall. Just then LC made out the silhouettes of two figures moving slowly toward them from the center of the mall. They were strange-looking, hunchbacked animals just like the ones LC and Gabby had seen in the woods. The two figures stopped when they got to the Little

Shop of Magic. LC nudged Gabby. "You were right!" he whispered.

One of the creatures lit a torch. The other got out a crowbar and proceeded to jimmy the lock on the door of the magic shop.

Suddenly the creatures looked over their shoulders as if they sensed someone was watching them. Their eyes rested right on the garbage can that LC and Gabby were hiding behind. LC froze. He crossed his fingers and hoped they couldn't hear his heart pounding.

"That doesn't make sense," whispered Gabby. "Why would they break into the Little Shop of Magic?"

At that moment a strange shrieking sound filled the air. Goose bumps crawled up and down LC's arms. Lights like fireworks suddenly lit up the area. At the same time, more hunchbacked animals appeared. They were everywhere!

"There go the gargoyles!" screamed Gabby as the strange silhouetted creatures shuffled forward, only half-visible in the glare of the showering lights.

All the officers popped out of their garbage cans.

"They went that way!" yelled Sergeant Pokey, pointing to the left.

The officers ran to the left as the creatures ran to the right.

"They're going the other way!" shouted Sergeant Pokey.

Some of the officers turned around and ran to the right.

"Get them, men!" yelled Sergeant Pokey.

But it was no use. The officers kept running into one another and grabbing at thin air. Before they knew what was happening, everything went dark again. The corridor was empty except for two of the creatures, who were lying on the floor, tangled up in each other's legs.

"Stop right there!" Sergeant Pokey commanded. "You're under arrest for breaking and entering, as well as for all of the other robberies in this mall and on Main Street."

The two figures stood up. They were holding gargoyle masks in their hands.

"But this is our first caper," said the taller one. "Honest."

"I told you these dumb gargoyle

costumes wouldn't work," said his shorter sidekick.

"I should have known," said Sergeant Pokey, clapping handcuffs on both of the men. "Tommy Too and Mac the Crack. You boys never learn, do you?"

"But Sergeant, I'm telling you—we just got these costumes," said the taller one.

"Tell it to the judge," said Sergeant Pokey, "but as far as I'm concerned, the citizens of Critterville can finally sleep in peace with you two no-goods behind bars."

"Sergeant Pokey," said Gabby, "maybe they're telling the truth. What about all those other gargoyles we saw? We better check out the Little Shop of Magic."

Before Sergeant Pokey could say anything, Gabby barged into the store.

"Gabby, they caught the thieves," said LC, following her. "Give it up already. L. B. Strangely and the gargoyles didn't commit the robberies."

But Gabby wasn't listening. She pushed open a door in the back of the shop.

"LC, come here!" she called.

LC walked into the room. In the center was a table covered with cards and candles. All the cards were facedown except for the one in the middle of the table. It was none other than the "SWYN . . . GARGOYLE OF GREED" card. And in each corner of the card were small splashes of color: one red, one green, one clear, and one blue.

"Okay, kids," called Sergeant Pokey. "It's time to go. You've been a big help."

"Sergeant Pokey," began Gabby, "this is the same card—"

"Sergeant!" one of the officers suddenly yelled, bursting into the shop. "The Gem Connection has been robbed. All the most valuable diamonds, rubies, emeralds, and sapphires are gone!"

"Tommy Too and Mac the Crack must have pulled off that one right before they came to this store," said Sergeant Pokey matter-of-factly.

"But, Sergeant," continued Gabby. "Where are all the stolen gems? How do you know they're really the robbers?"

Sergeant Pokey wasn't listening. He was already halfway out the door.

"See that Swyn card," said Gabby to LC, pointing to the table. "That's the same card that disappeared from your house. I told you L. B. Strangely took it."

"How do you know?" replied LC. "Maybe he has lots of cards like that."

"Maybe," said Gabby. "But I don't think so. And look carefully at the card. In the corner where there was a picture of a ruby is a red blob. Where there was a sapphire there's a blue blob. Where there was a diamond is a clear blob, and finally, where there was an emerald is a green blob."

"So?" said LC.

"So, I bet L. B. Strangely put a gemstone that he stole in each corner of this card," said Gabby. "And then he did some kind of magic trick that made the stones melt down into the strange blobs that are on this card right now!"

"That's ridiculous," said LC. "Those blobs are probably just wax. You have no proof that they were ever gems."

"But they *might* have been," said Gabby. "Now, do you notice anything interesting about where this Swyn card is positioned?"

"No," said LC.

"It's the only card that's faceup and it just happens to be in the center of the table, which corresponds exactly to the location of the Gem Connection in the mall," said Gabby. "And it just happens to be the one card that was missing last night when the other robberies occurred. And the one jewelry store that wasn't robbed then has now just been robbed."

"Okay, kids, let's go," said Sergeant Pokey. "There's nothing here. No gems. No gargoyles. This place is clean as a whistle."

"But what about those weird lights and those other gargoyles?" Gabby asked.

"That was just the emergency lighting system," said Sergeant Pokey. "Tommy and Mac shorted out the system with their blowtorch. And we didn't find any evidence of other gargoyles. Let's go."

LC and Gabby followed Sergeant Pokey and the other officers out of the mall.

"But, Sergeant—" Gabby began.

"The case is closed," Sergeant Pokey concluded firmly. "We caught the thieves. Now it's time to call it a night."

# CHAPTER 8

# NOW YOU SEE IT, NOW YOU DON'T!

The next Saturday afternoon, the Critter Kids were at the mall again. They were, as usual, trying to decide what to do.

"I'm telling you," Su Su said, "the dresses at Blueberries are to die for."

"I want to go to the bookstore," said Timothy. "I hear there's this new series called Magic Days and it's supposed to be lots of fun."

"What about the ice cream store?" suggested Henrietta. "I sure could go for a triple-scoop cone."

"I want to buy a pack of gum first," said Gabby, stopping at a candy and magazine shop. "Hey, guys, look at this!" she called, waving the *Critter Tribune* newspaper in the air.

All the Kids gathered around her. The headline of the paper read:

**JEWELRY STORE ROBBERIES AT RIVER'S EDGE MALL**

**ONLY EVIDENCE: THE SIGHTING OF DOGLIKE ANIMALS**

"I told you the guys at the stakeout didn't do it," said Gabby. "I told you it was L. B. Strangely and those gargoyles."

"Give me a break," said LC, shaking his head as he and the Critter Kids walked toward the escalator. "This is not a mystery like one of those Nancy Critter detective stories you're always reading. This is real life. And things like that don't happen in real life."

"Where is the Little Shop of Magic, anyway?" asked Velvet. "I thought it was right there next to that boutique."

"Me, too," said Gator.

"It was," said LC, walking up to the storefront next to the boutique. He peered inside. All the magic stuff was gone. The place was completely empty. A piece of paper was taped to the door. LC turned it over.

His eyes opened wide as he read the sign: "The Little Shop of Magic has moved. It is now located at the River's Edge Mall. Come see us there. Signed, L. B. Strangely."

The Critter Kids all looked at one another. Nobody said a word.